Before You Imagine,
Forget All You Know

A Collection of Fantasy
Short Stories and Poems

Written By:

Philip Lee McCall II

***

Cover By: Scott Messer

Best Wishes

Before You Imagine, Forget All You Know

Written By: Philip Lee McCall II

www.philipmccallii.com

www.mythixstudios.com

Edited By: Scott Humphries

www.scotthumphries.com

Cover By: Scott Messer

It has taken quite a bit of time, love and support to bring what you now hold in your hands to life. It is important that I thank those who helped me along this journey.

Thanks to my wonderful wife and muse Frances, who never would not let my dreams die, no matter how hard I (unknowingly) tried to let them.

Thanks to my editor Scott, for making this book better in prose and flow and reminding me that a writer was within me waiting to be heard.

Thanks to my dearest friends and very first fans. You fueled not only my writer's ego, but also my desire to let others see my creations.

To everyone who joined me on this journey, I send you my love and thanks with hope that you enjoy this little collection of my imagination.

~ PLMII

This book is dedicated to: *Stephanie*

Editor and friend, you shall be missed in this world.

Here is the book you asked for.

Before You Imagine, Forget All You Know

Before you imagine

Forget all you know

Let the journey begin

Away now you go

Through shadow and light

Curiosity amid a bit of fright

Accept as true this prose

See myth and legend

Exist in a wondrous land

Envisioned without end

By a simple writer's hand

A mind fills empty paper

Such a wondrous caper

Accept as true this prose

If you just believe

Trust in your mind's eye

These words shall conceive

A fantasy alive

Dragons shall take flight

In dark caverns torches light

Accept as true this prose

Before you imagine

Forget all you know

Let the journey begin

Away now you go

~

Succubi

Their laughter
Full of disaster
Leathery wings beat
As light does retreat

Fangs and fury
Horrid lustful squeals
In unholy glory
The dark reveals

Succubi, Succubi
Painful and passionate
Succubi, Succubi
Beauty's one regret
Succubi, Succubi
Cursed and cherished
Succubi, Succubi

Loved now perished

Succubi, Succubi

Tonight I die

In their den of lies

No chance to fly

No one hears my cries

Their skin alabaster

Cold as winter

A devilish treat

Without heartbeat

Fangs and fury

Horrid lustful squeals

In unholy glory

The dark reveals

Succubi, Succubi

Painful and passionate

Succubi, Succubi

Beauty's one regret

Succubi, Succubi

Cursed and cherished

Succubi, Succubi

Loved now perished

Succubi, Succubi

Tonight I die

In their den of lies

No chance to fly

No one hears my cries

~

Jack and Jill

Jack and Jill
Went up the hill
To fetch a pail of water
Their feast would be the best
Upon their unexpected guest
The foolish farmer's daughter

Jack heated up the pot
Jill threw in chilies not too hot
They dropped into their stew
Broken bone and tender sinew
They saved the rest for later
In vinegar and brown paper

~

Boo-Boo Black Demon

Boo, boo, black demon

Have you any spells?

Yes master, yes master

Three tomes full

One for the master

And one for the devil

And one for the little witch

Who lives down the lane

~

Moon Shift

Into the darkness I walked

Not sure where I had been

Lost among the evergreens

The moon on high

In a darkened sky

A curse deep in veins

The tear of flesh

And pale lace dress

A shape unforeseen

A hunger risen upon

Desire for innocence strong

Madness took me in

I ran free

I was not me

Lupine and hungry

~

Fields of Blood

Honor and solace

In the midst of war

Draped in bloodied gore

Screams all about

The glint of steel

The wind perfumed with death

For King!

For Land!

Upon ancient hand

Rise to battle!

Rage for more!

Death welcomed us all

~

Belladonna's Price

She rose to an erect position as the writhing crown of serpents morphed to a silken mane of ebon curls. Her once venomous tresses draped her pale nude form. The chill of the night air bit her skin as she dismounted her victim and robed her self in the fast chilling bed's linens. She shivered slightly and gazed upon the young man who now lay dead upon the bed. His face covered in vicious love bite marks, his skin now paling to a cold blue.

A smile crept to her lips like a mausoleum door opening. The young man, who sought a night of simple passion had found more than he bargained for, and now paid with his life. Belladonna giggled her body alive with the energy that once filled her victim. She dropped the linen and let the cool air wash over her bare form. Hers was a body of desire; its succulent shapes a fatal trap to any man who longed for her touch and embrace. She was a gorgon, a creature of villainous beauty and want. An appetite belonged to her race one sated only by the theft of another's life force.

She strode over to her victim, gloating at the effects of her feeding in its final phase. The man's corpse had begun to turn to stone. She reached over and caressed his chest, feeling the ice-cold hard granite. Belladonna turned away from him and dressed slowly luxuriating in the stolen life as it coursed through her body. She would not have to feed again for several weeks and she wanted to enjoy the fleeting moment.

***

Lord Arquinas gazed upon the voluptuous woman who sat in his private chambers. Her beauty was intoxicating and he struggled not to fall under her vile charms.

"So is he dead?" Arquinas question was barely a whisper.

"Yes, quite," Belladonna answered purring slightly.

Arquinas smiled with infamy, and suddenly laughed with sick joy. He sat in a plush chair and eagerly faced Belladonna. He longed to touch her, desiring to know her every inch of pale flesh. He knew this would mean his own death. She was a monster, but one that had served him well. His desire mixed with his horror, as he imagined, for a moment, what deathly pleasures she might give.

"Now that you have exacted your revenge upon the man who had lain with your wife, it is time to discuss my payment." Belladonna hissed as her eyes flash with desire.

"What I have asked for, you have delivered. Is one hundred coins sufficient?" Arquinas stood and walked to his coffer, his back turned to her, no doubt a dangerous gambit.

"Gold shall not cover this act I have completed for you, Milord."

Belladonna's answer stopped Arquinas in his tracks. He looked at her and quite suddenly, a chill ran up his spine. His mind raced franticly for a reward this creature could ask for in return for her deadly services. He did not think about it long, for she told him.

"Your wife carries a bastard child, this is what I desire." Belladonna's voice oozed with longing.

Arquinas stared at her in shock and horror, but then his fear evaporated. He smiled with an idea born in his mind. He would do away with the child his wife carried from a worthless serf, and ensure his bloodline remained true. He would also teach his loving wife from now on she should keep her passions to his bed. His mind pondered what the gorgon would do with this child but quickly pushed those thoughts aside. The bastard child's welfare was not his concern.

"My wife will not simply give up this child you desire," Arquinas stated with feigned concern.

"She will if you give her this." Belladonna produced a vial hidden within her dress. Arquinas's eyes strayed a bit too long on her low-cut blouse. He quietly realized his mistake and looked elsewhere. Belladonna sauntered over and placed the vial upon the Lord's desk.

"What is in that vial?" Arquinas asked the gorgon.

"A potion to help her slowly forget the child, when it's born, she will have no desire for it at all. Give the potion to her in small doses until the vial is empty. It carries no smell or taste when mixed with a strong brewed tea." Belladonna paused and looked at Arquinas, "When the birth is close, call for me once more and I shall act as nursemaid and relieve her of the unwanted child."

Arquinas sighed. He did not fully trust Belladonna, but he knew it was best not to cross her. The child, he reasoned was fair payment for his completed revenge. He picked up the vial. He stared shortly at it, mesmerized at the milky liquid that filled the glass shell.

He sighed, as if resigned to his fate. "Fine, your price shall be paid. Leave now and await my summons." Arquinas ordered his wicked guest.

Belladonna sensuously pulled up her hood, and turned to face Arquinas. A single black serpent slithered from under her hood, glassily gazing at the lord. He noticed that the gorgon's eyes had changed to match the exposed reptile.

She hissed warningly, "Do not consider betrayal of our pact Milord, my anger is like my passion.

Ssssomething not easily ssssated." She left without another word.

****

Arquinas had fulfilled the instructions Belladonna had left him. He had secretly administered the potion to his wife with her evening tea. Just weeks before the child entered the world, his wife's health had started to decline, Arquinas suspected the gorgon had tricked him and perhaps he had poisoned his wife. His court physician could not cure her sudden sickness, but told the lord the child within her womb seemed in fine health. He suggested that perhaps the birth would be difficult for her, but should not cause her death.

Arquinas was not convinced, and he summoned his guards to seek out Belladonna. She arrived to his home unescorted and Arquinas knew that he would never see the man who had found her.

"You have poisoned my wife, you bitch!"
Arquinas spat.

Belladonna laughed and sat in a nearby chair.
She tossed her head, sending a wave of curls to rush
about her shoulders.

"Milord, the birth of this bastard child may only
be taxing your loving wife. I assure you the potion
you gave her will not in any way bring about her
death." Belladonna informed Arquinas.

Arquinas momentarily quelled his anger. He
considered everything that had transpired and saw
that the gorgon would not gain by the death of his
wife if she desired the child. He still was concerned
his wife may not survive the birth, and for all his
desire for revenge, he could not fathom losing her.

"You will now attend to my wife in the final
stages of her deliverance of this child. Should she die I
will hold you responsible and our pact negated. You,

dear Belladonna, shall be executed for her murder," Arquinas stated with satisfaction.

"You worry too much Milord; I need your wife to live; she carries my child. Her death would serve me not." Belladonna stood and bowed to Arquinas. "I shall care for your wife and take my payment. There is no need for executions, there has already been enough death delivered from your hands, Arquinas." Belladonna left and sought out the Lord's wife.

***

Lady Gertrude looked pale and worn as she lay in her large bed. Belladonna washed her face with a cool rag and hummed a soft tune.

"Thank you Belladonna, your care has made these days easier to bear. " Gertrude said with a tremendous sigh. She felt so weak as if her life drained from her with every breath.

"Sometimes I think this child will be the death of me. Perhaps the Gods seek to punish me for my sins." Gertrude cried out.

Belladonna brushed the Lady's damp hair away from her face and smiled innocently. As Belladonna cared for her, the Lady of the house had instantly taken to her new nursemaid, speaking often of her most inner thoughts.

"Such foolish talk Milady, what ever could such a beautiful and loving wife as you do to bring the Gods' wrath?" Belladonna asked, fully knowing to what Gertrude referred.

"My dear can you keep a secret?" Gertrude asked, her voice desperate.

"I can for you Milady."

"The child I carry is not of my husband; I have lain with another man, and now shall bear his child." Gertrude gasped for air, as birthing pain suddenly wracked her weak body.

Belladonna noticed the child's coming and prepared the mother. She shouted to a guard outside the Lady's chambers to retrieve a barrel of water and returned to Gertrude who now screamed with pain. She spoke gently to Gertrude, telling her to urge the child forward. The Lady's sweating legs quivered violently and slipped in Belladonna's grasp. The gorgon gripped them once more and spread them apart. She yelled for Gertrude to help the child enter the world.

"Help me! The child brings me pain!" Gertrude screamed.

Belladonna ignored her pleas as she saw the babe emerge from within her mother's flesh. She reached in and gently turned the child's bloody head as each strain from its mother pushed it slowly out. Belladonna filled with excitement and joy. Gertrude's child was about to be hers forever.

Gertrude's agonizing screams filled the room, her body jerked violently and then became still. The cries of a newborn child filled the air. Belladonna gazed upon the host of her child, whose skin gave off a bluish tint. The birth had not killed her, the child had. The vile of gorgon venom her husband has given her, had altered her unborn child and made it a gorgon. It had fed within the womb upon its motherly host.

Arquinas burst into the room, his eyes fell upon Gertrude and his face went pale. His hands shook with rage and loss as he closed the door and lowered the brace to lock it.

"You lied to me. You have slain my wife, you vile and wicked whore!" Arquinas spat and unsheathed his sword. He would finish this madness now and kill Belladonna and her ill-gotten child.

"You sought revenge through murder and call me the villain? How odd that is Milord. This wife of yours has done me a favor and given me a child that I could never have." Belladonna smiled as she held the babe in her arms, covered in her mother's blood.

"You and your misbegotten child shall pay with your lives for what you have done. I shall finish this myself." Arquinas moved upon Belladonna, his weapon held dangerously in his pale and trembling hands.

Belladonna hissed and took a defensive stance cradling the child. Her beautiful mane writhed to reptilian life and each snake head struck out in anger toward Arquinas. Her eyes flashed with pure hatred and she leapt with blinding speed away from Arquinas as he sought to strike her down with his blade.

"Call for your guards Arquinas if you wish to live. You are no match for me!" Belladonna growled.

"I need no one to end this evil I have created, wretched wench!" Arquinas moved in and attacked once more. Belladonna twisted in an unnatural way. It was then Arquinas realized her legs now replaced with that of a serpent's body. The gorgon rose up and struck fast. Arquinas fell, unprepared for such an unnatural act. She held him up, as he screamed.

The Lord writhed in the air as serpents tore through his face and devoured his life force. Moments later, Belladonna dropped Arquinas's mutilated corpse to the floor, shifting back to a more human appearance. The child in her arms wriggled and cried out. A motherly smile crossed her lips.

"Are you hungry my child?" She cooed and lowered her blouse to expose her breast. Gently she raised the child to her bare chest. Pain racked her bosom as she felt the small fangs sink deep.

"Feed my darling and grow strong. One day my love, I shall tell you how your father died and how good it was to devour him." Belladonna laughed and gently rocked the child in her arms.

The Guardsman of Arquinas broke into the Lady's chambers hours later to discover their Master and his wife turned to stone. The child and its nursemaid long vanished.

Later, travelers to the lands once ruled by Arquinas, told tales of a mother and daughter so beautiful, that no man alive could resist.

Hunter

A blade of silver
A blessed crucifix
All for when
I am in a fix

A trail of terror
Villager's faces pale
I listen with intention
To each and every tale

A feeling lingers
Upon every word
Their tales of horror
Not a bit absurd

A single prayer
Before I take leave

Of the Lord's protection

Less evil deceive

A wooden stake

A vial of holy water

Tools of my trade

For Evil's slaughter

Now I go alone

Forward to my fate

To the den of darkness

Beyond Nosferatu's gates

~

The Raven and the Scorpion

One day while flying in search of a meal, a raven spotted a scorpion crawling upon the rocks below. The raven flew down upon the scorpion intent upon the kill. The scorpion turned and his raised stinger.

"Spare me this day and I shall one day this life debt repay," said the scorpion.

The raven cawed and considered his meal's gesture. The raven agreed to the terms and took flight once more.

Seasons passed and the raven flew over the scorpion once more and descended to speak with him.

"Dear scorpion, I have need of you to slay my rival." The raven said with malice.

The scorpion agreed to fulfill his promise and asked the raven to take him upon his back to allow him quick passage to his rival. The raven bowed his head and the scorpion climbed upon his back.

"Why do you wish to kill your rival?" The scorpion asked the raven.

"Because I seek his flock and his nest, among us all it is the very best," replied the raven to his assassin.

The scorpion suddenly struck the raven with his stinger. The raven fell to the ground as poison coursed through his veins.

"Why have you done this? You owed me your life?" The raven cried his eyes clouding with death.

"I have given you this and now my debt repaid a life restored this day."

One does not save a life and ask one taken.

Virgin's Death

A virgin's touch

Upon silken mane

Innocence lost

The tap of hooves

In shadowed meadow

Surrounded by ancient mist

Eyes watch with greed

Upon the pale steed

Life worthless

The sharp snap of bowstring

A young girl's scream

Temptation of gold's gleam

Now stilled, lies the silken mane,

With the virgin's bloody stain

~

The Bard

The weep of lyre

Flicker of amber fire

Song upon lips pale

Melodic battle and death

With each rhythmic breath

Listen now and forget never

A crowd embraced

Tears line each face

A song for all to hear

A sweep of hand

Illusion forever grand

All for room and ale

~

Ned

Poor, little Ned was dead

He knew it in his hollow head

How he missed conversations

And often gave salutations

As he strolled in the park

Under the moon in the dark

With a cheerful boney little wave

As he wandered back to his grave

He would offer a friendly "Hi"

To any living passerby

They would scream with fright

In the dark of the night

To see an undead little boy

Never brought the living joy

Always in fear they ran away

Much to Ned's utter dismay

No matter how hard he would try

No one ever told him "Goodbye"

~

Shadow Kiss

Uncloaked in night

Beyond the sun

Forever death

Forever living

Seductive and alluring

A curse sought by many

The beat of a heart

In endless darkness

Red life

Warm drink

Love twisted and cruel

Taste beyond rules

Touch cold and ancient

Bitten with pain passionate

Given freely

To shadow

~

Silver Songbird

Hammer in hollow

Breath of swallow

Song from steel

Wings golden shimmer

Feathered in silver

Song from steel

Melodic and mystic

Flight of metal

Song from steel

A birth

A soaring symphony

Song from steel

~

In The Dell

In flight so bright

From flower to flower

Under green leaf and ancient rocky tower

A myth and a dream lives!

Dances upon fresh spring dew

Life and power anew

Innocence and fragility

Shimmering gossamer wings

Eyes the blackest of things

Mischief and mayhem

Laughter like silver bells

Deep in shadowed emerald dell

They frolic in the air

Full of mirth and glee

In the kingdom of fairy

~

The Hunt of the Unicorn

The moon's light poured gently through the forest canopy, as the animals of the forest crept about. The predators of the forest listened to the wind for the slightest movement, while the prey held its breath avoiding detection. A game of silence and death played its continuous cycle amongst the ancient oaks. Suddenly with out warning, the winds foretold of danger, the forest now no longer safe, sanctuary sullied. The hunt of the unicorn had begun.

The queen of the forest smelled them on the wind, heard their voices echoing in the cold night air. The invisible hands of fear touched her spine sending chills throughout her body, her muscles tensed instinctively and her nostrils snorted in the fine mist. The unicorn's eyes searched the trees for the intruders; she must know what shape death might chose to hunt her this night. The animals of the forest scurried, darting for cover, while the unicorn galloped off to a nearby hill to see her enemy.

Four humanoid shapes crept through the trees. They carried no torches but she could see their red eyes glowing in the darkness. She recognized the goblins by their scent as they entered the forest. Their dark intentions hung about their heads like ill-fitting, rotting skins. They wished to kill her and take her horn.

They would have to catch her first. She reared up, bayed, and called them to the chase.

The vile creatures grunted and ran in pursuit of the fleeing unicorn. Arrows rained within the canopy of shadowed green; swiftly the prey avoided their deadly touch. She could feel the wind dance rhythmically through her silken mane. Hooves clicked sharply in the shadows as she quickly darted across a small forest path. The screams of the goblins sang of frustration and the willingness to continue the chase.

The ancient oaks watched in horror as the goblins pursued the unicorn with a thirst for blood unmatched by any forest predator. Death laughed on the wind, as it blew through the trees. The unicorn shot through the forest on fiery hooves, like a comet. The hunters continued their grueling pace, firing arrows at the magical beast, taunting each other as they missed. None of the shards of death seemed to find their mark, but the hunt continued. She felt the burning in her lungs and the chill of cold sweat line her body. Halting to gain her bearings, she noticed the goblins had come over a nearby hill. They grunted and motioned to her, thinking they had cornered their quarry. They wore their false pride like bright tin armor. Once more, the unicorn reared defiant and proud. The sound of fired bows rang out, but the arrows struck only the ground where the magical beast had last stood.

Storm clouds gathered, dousing the moon's light and rumbled like war drums in the sky. Lightning struck a worn dead tree, bursting it into flames. The air grew hot and moist, announced the rain would soon come. Still the unicorn ran on the thrill of the pursuit coursed like raw fire through her veins. The hunters pace had slowed as they gasped for air and rubbed sore muscles. In anger, they looked about for their prey. The goblins examined the dark forest surroundings.

A primordial dance had begun, as the treetops swayed in unison under the weight of the growing winds. Some of the goblins announced their desire to end the futile hunt, while the majority silenced their cries and moved on.

The unicorn watched their movements from a small ledge, covered in wild grass and flowers. They had almost given up, but their evil goal had goaded them to continue. The goblins followed her tracks hoping to catch a glimpse of her. She was tired and knew if the goblins continued the hunt, sunlight would never frolic in her mane again. The unicorn felt old and a bit worn, but she would not let death take her so easily. She reared up, mocked her hunters and death, as the arrows tore through the turbulent wind. One of the arrows almost found its deadly mark. The unicorn snorted in disbelief and sprinted off. The goblins screamed as they chased her.

Fear crept like an unwelcome guest into her heart. She felt the cold touch of death reach for her once more. She galloped faster through the lush forest, and outrun fear to leave it behind in the dark. In the sky, dark clouds churned and rumbled like a witch's brew. Soon the spell of rain would be completed and fall upon the earth. The goblins continued their chase, sensing the unicorn's fear. This could mean only one thing she was beginning to tire. They would have their prize soon if they did not give up. One of the vile creatures blew a horn to raise the moral of his fellow hunters. The goblin bows sang again, the shafts took flight still unable to deliver death to their prey.

The moon fought in vain to pierce the dark clouds, under the violent ebony sky blanket. The hunt continued, prey running with death just upon its heels. The forest animals could not help but watch the mad race go on. They felt pain for the unicorn, which had protected them so long. Tonight they lay hidden unmarked by death, only the queen of the forest was and in a way, they were thankful. Somewhere in their minds they knew, her sacrifice would save so much more.

How free she felt as the midnight air, raced upon her body as she ran. The energy of youth was returning to her old body, she knew this might be the last hunt. The unicorn snorted the thought away; the goblins would have to kill her first. She slowed to a trot and looked back down the hill; the goblins struggled to keep up. Their screams came between their gasps for air, and the futile attempts to fire arrows upon her. The unicorn knew just over the hill lay her salvation. Many moons ago an old tree had fallen across a gorge, creating a natural bridge. She planned to cross the log. Then kick the old fallen tree into the deep ravine below. The goblins would have no way across. They would have to head back to find a way across, by then she would be far from their clutches. The rain began to fall in waves from the sky, the unicorn bolted up the hill.

The goblins clamored upon the hill. They spotted the unicorn as she headed for the gorge. They could see a tree stretched across it, and one of them screamed to fire their bows. Arrows took flight but the unicorn was too fast. The old tree lay just ahead and the unicorn summoned all her strength to dash across. The sky above shook in anger and a bolt of lightning shot out of the heavens. The fallen tree could not handle the lightning strike; it began to snap in half. The unicorn reared up and bayed in fright, regained her wits, leaped back to the hill and the waiting goblins. There was no way out now, the bloodthirsty goblins stood bows notched. The unicorn reared in defiance, and in the sky, lightning flashed lighting the forest for all to see death standing upon the hill. Arrows zipped through the rain as the unicorn charged the goblins.

Death embraced the queen of the forest, as her body fell to the ground. The unicorn could hear the goblins scream for joy, as death's cold grasp pulled her slowly away. She would run now with the herd across the sky. Like all of her kind she knew, one day she would not get away. The goblins could have her horn; her passing has saved so much more.

The morning sun chased the storm clouds away, shining upon the animals of the forest gathered around their fallen queen. Predator and prey sat together mourning the passage of their monarch.

Suddenly a white form burst from nearby brush, sending the animals scattering. A young unicorn trotted up to the fallen queen, her mother. She touched her small horn, to the stump where her mother's used to be. The animals sounded off, as the new queen raised her small head. There would be no tears for the young monarch. She knew one day hunters would seek her, but they would have catch her first. The young queen reared in defiance ran off into the ancient green forest.

Beside the River

Forever he goes to the river
To lay his tears to rest
Beside the running blue water
Lay the prices of a broken trust

It was so many years ago
And only the wind truly knows
The forgotten tale of two lovers
Who proclaimed their love by the river

Once beneath the moon and stars
Love left its terrible and unforgotten scar
Upon two young loving hearts
Whose once sweet world has fallen apart

So night after night, he comes to cry
Talk to memories and ask why

That a love said to last forever

Became a sacrifice upon an unseen altar

Beneath the stars

Beside the river

Underneath the moon

She was young

Full of life

And ever so fair

She dreamed

She loved

She danced upon air

She the beauty fair

Belongs in his longing arms

Not in an unknown writer's song

Fate can be so cruel

As it plays by self made rules

It came like a thief in the night

Among the shadows far from sight

With tainted dagger, it slew true love

Like a pure white sacrificial dove

She was alone under obsidian sky

As death the collector came

Forever she closed her eyes

Beneath the stars

Beside The River

Underneath the moon

How quickly death slipped away

After her soul was set free

Before the sun claimed a new day

It was then her lover
Came upon her skin so cold and pale
He knew he would never know the tale

So he gave her to the churning river
Upon a handmade raft full of flowers
Mother Nature took away the empty shell
Far away, a soul stood judgment in hell

A thousand years have come and gone
Yet his soul's lamentation far from done
He sits alone endlessly in ghostly tears
Lost everything he considered so dear

And you the reader must wonder why
Why his soul returns endlessly to cry
Nightly beside the lonely river
His lover's reflection haunts the water
So together he and she

Must live out endless misery

They see each other so much

Yet alas, they never touch

For if, he reaches to touch her face

The sweet longing reflection separates

She leaves without a trace

And the night how it grows ever late

Two worn spirits fill with endless hate

As the murderer remains ever free

Their eyes shall never see

Beneath the stars

Beside the river

Underneath the moon

So, I lay down my pen

And remember the murder again

I saw the terror in her eyes

As I heard her futile cries

My dagger slide in

I committed my sin

Beneath the stars

Beside the river

Underneath the moon

You say I am a murderer

My words untrue

She was alive until you read

You are the true murderer

No one killed her but you

Beneath the stars

Beside the river

Underneath the moon

I wrote these words you have read

Now too my words done

I am dead

~

Beautiful Death

Dammar's hands paused in concentration, as the ground around him groaned in agony. Ancient bones of heroes or perhaps villains long dead sprouted like newborn flowers of death from the soil. The necromancer laughed with a deep guttural sound, directly at the red-haired woman facing him. Her hands danced rhythmically as she struggled to summon the strength of the world around her. Undead groaned as they emerged ever higher from the earth and mocked her with empty voices. A cold wind began to pick up all about her as leaves swirled in the air.

"It is over, Sosanna. You are all that blocks my path to greatness, and now you, too, shall die protecting this place." Dammar screamed and cackled once more as the skeletons now rose to their full height around him. They stared through dark eye sockets at the druid, and their jaws chattered noisily. She refused to falter. Dammar would meet the master he chose to follow; even if she must journey to Death's waiting arms with him.

"Chikaos –Temzala "Sosanna shouted. Her voice resonated like booming thunder in the air. The skeletons surrounding the necromancer shattered, white dust and bone shards littering the air about the combatants. A curse followed by choking announced the necromancer was not pleased with this sudden turn of events not in his favor.

Dammar regained his composure, black evil spewed from his mouth. Eerie blue light surrounded his form, and his voice suddenly began echoing murky chants from the spirits of long-dead elders. Sosanna felt life ebb from her body, her mind slowly grasping the situation.

A life-stealing charm was draining her energy faster than sand through an hourglass. Frantic thoughts tumbled into her hazed mind; she searched to form the words for a defense. Laughter, the hated sound of her enemy rang in her ears. It was his attempt to distract her. Confusion littered her consciousness, but she sensed the need to regain control before life emptied from her body. Grass beneath her feet wilted brown, she struggled, and a cold sweat quickly drenched her skin. Incantations left her trembling lips, energy streamed into her spirit, and a scream ripped the air as Dammar doubled over in pain. The tables were now turned; the dead grass about the druid bloomed green and alive. Sosanna took the upper hand and unleashed her fury; thorns ripped through pallid flesh as agony bore tears the color of blood to the necromancer's eyes.

"Semxos," he spat the word, and its effect was immediate. Her hold loosened its grip upon him.

His flesh torn and bleeding, it seared with pain, and slowly a sly smile crept over his pale face.

"Well done, Druid, though it has gained you naught." His hands fluttered, shadows gathered in his grip and he flung them at his opponent. Sosanna was unprepared, and the silk like strands bound her arms to her side. Fortune had changed sides once again.

Dammar surveyed his apparent victim with a calculated stare full of hatred, animosity and pleasure. This game, he felt, was at an end; there was a world to enslave, and it was time that this druid and her dearly departed cohorts vacate his path to supreme power. He summoned from deep within the ultimate forbidden magic, more than enough vile strength to deal with his hampered enemy. Sosanna fought the dark bonds; her spirit appeared to give up all hope for the world and her survival. Her enemy's spell had power over her body but not her mind.

"Hilas-Boreuas," the charm snarled from her dry lips, shadows faltered, freedom returned. Sosanna just managed to duck under the bolt of iridescent green lightening, which zoomed past her, shot from the necromancer's gnarly fingers. She now understood how the others of her order had perished; this man was powerful and carried death in him like clouds full of rain. Deep within her mind a thought came to life, it was a prayer and a curse bonded in eternal dance. Rain of death must never fall again; a vessel to hold it forever trapped was the answer and the victory she sought. The druid cast a protective shield about herself; Dammar's non-stop attacks bounced off the invisible barrier, unable to penetrate.

"You are weak like the others," he raged, "And I will cherish your death." He bared his teeth and a wave of spells followed.

Sosanna's barrier would not hold much longer, she had to act with speed. A series of incantations danced on her sweet voice, and amber light pulsed from her entire body, growing greater in strength with each passing moment. She began to feel the heart of the earth as it beat in time with her own. Tears rolled down the planes of her face. She knew there could be no return from this path, no absolution for the sacrifice she was about to commit. A protector of life would not seek the destiny she chose now in one fatal moment. The faces of her dead friends dissolved to distant, faded images as her mind, which now burned with virtuous flames hot, powerful, and ancient. Dammar reserved in his attack, unaware of what was transpiring deep within the druid. Sosanna dropped the barrier; her eyes pulsed with the gleaming amber light that covered her shaking form.

"I shall not let your darkness embrace the world, but my soul will embrace your darkness forever!"

Sosanna shrieked, dazzling light engulfed both druid and necromancer, and Dammar let out a blood-curdling scream of helpless surprise. Unthinkable pain racked his body, and his limbs ceased to function.

Sosanna's soul writhed in agony, as Dammar's evil life force entered. Amber brilliance filled the air, and hummed deep with fury. The druid and necromancer merged, and she took control the bearer of life and death. Lifeless Dammar's twisted body fell with a thud to the forest floor. Finally, the amber light was gone leaving only the druid with red hair kneeling upon the ground, her skin pale as first winter's snow.

She could feel his tortured consciousness deep within her, his vile energy coursing throughout her veins. Trembling she rose. Plant life around her died and turned black. Tears, once more, lined her face.

Never again would life long for her touch. Animals would feel her presence and run. Sosanna staggered slowly out of the forest she once protected, leaving a trail of death and destruction wherever she stepped. This was her choice. Gifted beyond anyone he had ever seen her Master had declared long ago, Sosanna did not feel gifted any longer. Cursed she was and would forever be, but the world was safe through her sacrifice. The knowledge of this act would be the one cherished memory to bring her solace on long cold nights to come.

Years waned. Travelers everywhere spoke of a beautiful, red-haired woman wandering in the deserts far to the south. They said her eyes were dark and troubled. She spoke of a forest loved and missed, and would ask everyone she met how the flowers smelled after the first spring rain.

Mother Goose

Wicked Mother Goose

Loved her silken noose

And delighted in whips and chains

While in her dungeon

She would often bludgeon

Those who sought their way

Upon her black stilettos

She laughed in the dark grotto

With every victim's scream of pain

One is required to behave

In the Wicked Mother's cave

For she shall make you pay

~

Little Boy Blue

Little Boy Blue lives all alone
Among cadavers, sinew and bone
He paints their faces with a bright smile
To look alive for just a while

With shovel digs their final place
Families then come to his place
With tears in their eyes
For those who die

He dresses fair
With curly golden hair
In suit of indigo hue
Hence, they call him, Little Boy Blue

~

Weasel and the Rabbit

A weasel had fallen to a hunter's trap and cried out in pain. A rabbit heard his cry and came out of curiosity to seek its source. The weasel spotted the rabbit and called to him.

"Dear friend rabbit, like a fool I have fallen to this trap of man. Would you not lend me a hand and set me free of it," the weasel begged.

The rabbit hopped closer and saw the weasel's hind leg seized in the metal jaws of the trap.

"Help you say, from me this day, my question this to you, if you found me this way, would you help or feast upon me?" The rabbit asked.

The weasel smiled as best he could and understood the rabbit's frame of mind.

"Dear rabbit, the truth of that is unforeseen, but now I face death from man our mutual enemy. Please hurry I will not seek your harm, release me from this prison of mine."

The rabbit considered the weasel's words and knew them partially true. The weasel was wounded and perhaps not a threat. Then he moved in and with his hind legs opened the jaws of man's death cage.

The weasel suddenly sprung upon his savior. The hare looked up in horror.

"Thank you my friend, now I shall return the favor and not let you linger, and your flesh I shall relish," the weasel growled with delight.

"You promised not to harm me should I set you free," squealed the rabbit.

"Understand you not the rules of prey and predator?"

The weasel began to laugh aloud, but then he stooped and jerked away from his prey. The rabbit scrambled to his feet and looked into the eyes of a fox. The weasel lay limp in the fox's jaws. The fox growled a warning. The rabbit needed no further instruction and hopped away to safer grounds.

An enemy in peril is still thy enemy once in safety

Jack

Jack is nimble

Jack is quick

Jack is an arsonist

With torch in hand

Amber flames to command

He lit many a blazing fire

But then one day

The wicked flames did stray

Their master sought to get away

Jack was nimble

Jack was quick

However, the flames were quicker

~

Old King Cole

Old King Cole was a wicked old soul,

Moreover, a wicked old soul was he

He called for his axe,

And he called for his executioner,

In addition, he called for his prisoners three

Every prisoner had committed no crime,

No crimes at all had he, had he

Set us free, set us free, went the prisoners three

The King smiled wickedly grand

With royal flair raised his hand

Off went their heads one, two, and three

Old King Cole was a wicked old soul,

Moreover, a wicked old soul was he

He called for his axe,

And he called for his executioner,

He never set a prisoner free

~

Smith of Promise

Hammer, chisel and forge

For ancient king

Hammer, chisel and forge

In fire's glimmer

In heat's embrace

Shaping metal's face

Hammer, chisel and forge

For ancient queen

Hammer, chisel and forge

A lover's will

Through dwarven skill

A dream fulfilled

Hammer, chisel and forge

Rings wrought

Shimmer of diamond caught

Forever bound together

Entwined in gold and silver

For ancient king to ancient queen

Love promised in metal sheen

Hammer, chisel and forge

~

Magi Duel

A flick of the wrist

A twist of the tongue

Just a pinch of sulfur

The magic has begun

Shimmering Flame

Dances upon flesh

Roaring with natural power

Against its arcane master

Through the air

An amber deadly dance

The intended recipient

Bares little chance

Apprentice to master

The game unfolds

A challenge accepted

From youth so bold

A flick of the wrist

A twist of the tongue

Just a pinch of sulfur

An the game is done

~

A Guest for Dinner

Moonlight spilled down upon the shadowy streets of the great city of Blodstad. North of the trade city called Caliburg and west of Anitiqar Sea, Blodstad was a dangerous bustling city. Dark deals and death pacts were made within its stone walls. Still, this put no damper on the amount of trading that went on in the city's large marketplace. Blodstad, nicknamed "Anitiqar's gem", was the singular city where one could find anything his or her heart desired. Home to many wealthy Lords and Ladies, it was a prime target for those who sought to gain from other's coffers.

The City Guard, well-armed and paid well too occasionally look the other way, kept the city relatively safe.

Life in Blodstad was good and profitable, so the minor inconvenience of thievery and assassination was overlooked. Profit ruled this city and as long as the gold coins kept flowing, little else mattered.

***

The small shop known as Whisperstone's Wonders, sat deep within Blodstad's northern corner. The people of Blodstad referred to this part of the city as "Thief Town". The shop's owner cared not what his neighbors called this section of the city. He was making money. If he dealt with some shady characters, he figured such was the price of gaining wealth.

Angus Whisperstone was one of the few dwarves who ran a shop within Blodstad; his namesake carried everything, and anything a respectable rogue could ever want. The dwarf stroked his finely combed black beard as he hunched over the day's sales figures. He grinned noting he had sold twenty daggers today; thieves were a profitable group of customers. He reasoned that if they continued to stab each other in the back as often as they did, he would be in business for a very long time. There was a sudden explosion from a room in the back of his shop. Angus looked up from his work and rolled his eyes in frustration. A small figure emerged from the back, his small cloth apron still smoldering from recently being on fire. His face covered in black soot, and he grinned at Angus sheepishly.

"I hope you didn't destroy my forge and you put any fires out, Servis." Angus cautioned, trying not to laugh.

"Yes, I was the only thing on fire, Master Whisperstone, "Servis replied, rubbing his hands on his scorched apron

"It is a good thing you gremlin shave your heads and beards. You would have burned yourself alive by now, "Angus commented while focusing back on his work.

Servis was a gremlin. He was the best gremlin Angus had ever known. That was the reason why the dwarf had hired him. Gremlins by nature are a peaceful race, but ironically their skills are known as the birthplace of many a mechanized weapon, or tool of destruction. The gremlin built contraptions of all sorts; sometimes they worked, and sometimes a gremlin became a victim of his own bad invention. Most Dwarves shunned their oddities, and could not understand why any gremlin would shave off his lovely beard. A well-kept beard made a dwarf who he was, but gremlins shunned this concept. The gremlin had their own guilds within many cities; the location of their fatherland was a mystery to all who lived in the known world. Angus, while on a visit to his homeland, had purchased a crossbow. When he inquired about the maker of the fine weapon, he was taken to meet Servis Rockspring. The dwarf liked Servis from the start. The gremlin was respectful, and worked wonders with his deft hands. Angus left the dwarven city with Servis in tow. The young gremlin agreed to work for Angus in return for a share of the store's profits and a workshop of his own. Angus had once asked Servis why he shaved his head and beard. The gremlin stated it was for safety reasons. Angus, having seen Servis as the cause a few disasters within his own shop, did not argue the point.

"Well, Servis, clean up the forge area and your newest invention. I am almost done with these numbers, then I'm going to lock up, "Angus stated while adding up the day's profits.

"Yes Master Whisperstone, "Servis shouted over his shoulder as he ran to clean up his mess.

Angus looked up from his work to see his friend run to the back of the shop. The dwarf smiled and then chuckled softly. He liked the young inventor, even if he was a gremlin. Servis worked hard, and if his inventions didn't work all the time, he was still the best friend anyone could have. The bell that hung just above the door to the shop rang. Angus wished he had locked the door earlier. He put down his papers and went to inform his late customer that the shop was closed. The dwarf arrived at the front of the shop to find it empty and the door closed. He scratched his chin and looked about. There appeared to be nothing missing, and he proceeded to walk over and lock the door. The dwarf figured some drunk had opened the door by mistake. He locked the door, but he still felt something was wrong. Angus shrugged his suspicions off and went back to finish his work. He stopped to blow out the front lantern. This way there could be no confusion to the passerby that his shop was closed.

****

He watched the dwarf head to the back of the shop and without a sound jumped from behind a tall shelf. The figure moved swiftly and followed his victim. He watched as the dwarf sat at his desk and began to pore over his paper work. The intruder smiled, this was going to be so easy.

Angus looked up; he thought he heard something in the room. The dwarf's tired eyes scanned the room; he saw nothing out of the ordinary. He told himself, that he was not about to get touchy about a bump in the night. Suddenly something grabbed him from behind. The dwarf gasped and twisted around to greet a huge grin from a face the dwarf knew all too well.

"Adaxxis Nightshade, have you lost your mind? You almost scared the honesty completely out of me! "The dwarf blustered, trying to gain a measure of his lost composure, and let his guest know how rude it is to sneak up on people.

"You should thank me then, Angus, " the pale elf named Adaxxis stated with a laugh.

"Thank you why?" Angus shot back at his visitor.

"Someone as despicable as you can't live with an ounce of honesty in him." The dwarf's guest started to laugh once more.

Angus eyed the assassin, snorted and called Servis from the back of the shop. The gremlin came running wearing a new apron and most of the soot cleaned from his face. Upon seeing Adaxxis he shot a huge grin and ran to greet him.

"Mister Nightshade, how wonderful it is to see you again, "Servis beamed, heartily shaking Adaxxis's pale hand. Adaxxis smiled and proceeded to retrieve his hand from the over friendly gremlin.

"It is good to see you too, Servis, is my crossbow ready?" the assassin asked politely, with wide grin.

"Well, Servis don't stand there. Get the elf his crossbow. "Angus shouted to his friend, who was not answering. The gremlin nodded and left, almost tripping in his haste.

Angus looked over at Adaxxis; the elf's eyes were orange in color. The dwarf had never seen any living being with eyes like Adaxxis; then again, he had never quite met anyone like him either. The assassin was average height for an elf, and he was what other elves must have considered extremely handsome. Angus had seen many the elven and human female get quite silly upon seeing Adaxxis. The odd thing was his skin was so milky-white and pale. Angus had never seen anyone like that, though he had heard tales of such beings, Naga they were called. The legend stated they had pale skin, red eyes and white hair. Adaxxis had long straight raven black hair just brushing his shoulders and his eyes were orange in color not red at all. The Naga were known to be extremely evil, the stuff of nightmares to most living beings, that is the few who had the good fortune of living after encountering them in the flesh. The dwarf had never pried into the elf's personal history or affairs, so he knew only what the assassin told him. Angus felt that if Adaxxis wanted him to know something he would tell him.

"Angus how is business?" the assassin asked while mindlessly spinning a dagger upon his palm.

"Good, though I have a few contracts open. Would you be interested? "Angus responded.

"What do you have?" The assassin stood up and walked over to the dwarf's desk.

The dwarf rummaged through some scrolls upon his desk, looking at each one. He handed the assassin a scroll after a few minutes of searching through his cluttered desk. Adaxxis read the scroll intently and then rolled it up and handed it back to Angus.

"What is the offer?" Adaxxis asked the dwarf.

"The request is for a Well-known, are you up for that?" The dwarf questioned Adaxxis, and raised an eyebrow.

"Angus, I am fully aware that an assassination in front of a room full of people is dangerous, "Adaxxis remarked slyly.

Angus knew that the elf was aware of the term Well-known. The killing of a Mark out in the open was dangerous and if he succeeded, he would be hunted for quite a while. The City Guard did not take kindly to open displays of murder for hire. He just wanted to be sure that Adaxxis was comfortable with the ramifications of the job.

"Okay, the payment is two hundred gold coins." The dwarf stated, and waited for the elf's response.

"Agreed, I will need a layout of the manor for the about-to-be dearly departed Lord Jennithos. "Adaxxis smiled noting that Servis had returned carrying a small box.

The gremlin opened the box for the assassin to look inside, a small crossbow sat within the box. It looked well made and quite deadly in the right hands. Adaxxis removed the crossbow, which felt light even with a bolt already in it. He aimed the crossbow at Angus who was busy searching a shelf for the information on the Lord Jennithos's manor. The elf was pleased with the weapon and placed it back in the box. The gremlin smiled, removed the crossbow from the box again, and held it up for Adaxxis.

"Here, just next to the trigger, is a lever. When the lever is up it is on safety and will not fire, "the gremlin stated.

"I see. That is quite a good feature, Servis. "Adaxxis nodded.

"If the safety is not on, like this, and is fired, " the gremlin sneezed suddenly and there was a twang as the crossbow fired. The bolt shot across the room. Servis could not bear to look, upon hearing Angus yelp loudly. The gremlin could hear Adaxxis laughing, and could feel Angus's blood begin to boil within the room.

"Servis, have you lost your mind?" Angus shouted with his long beard pinned to the bookshelf by a small crossbow bolt. The dwarf's face was red with embarrassment and anger. The gremlin ran over and proceeded to help his friend free his beard from the bookshelf. The dwarf began to swat at the gremlin, and yanked the bolt free.

"You almost killed me, you dunder-head. Go back to the forge before I really get angry, "Angus shouted and pointed to the back of the shop. The gremlin bowed and ran off, apologizing the whole way. Angus picked up a map from the floor, handed it and the bolt to the assassin.

"Well, if I do make any enemies, and they want me killed, they can hire Servis and save themselves some money. That fool of a gremlin is dangerous, but he still is the best friend anyone can have, "Angus grunted feeling a bit sorry for shouting at his young friend.

"Perhaps you should tell him that, " Adaxxis remarked while looking over the map.

Angus snorted and knew the elf was right. He called Servis back up front. The gremlin crept up a few minutes later and looked down at the floor while addressing Angus.

"Yes Master Whisperstone, "Servis stated softly.

"Servis, you can't go around killing your friends. It puts a damper on the friendship. I think you are a good blacksmith, but you must be careful. "Angus patted Servis on the shoulder and smiled. The gremlin proceeded to grab and shake Angus's hand quite frantically.

"Thank you, Master Whisperstone." The gremlin shouted, and continued to shake Angus's hand.

"Yes, yes, now run along and get ready to close up, "Angus replied while removing his hand from the excited gremlin's grasp.

Servis bolted to the back of the shop, glad that Angus respected his skills and still considered him a friend. Angus was right. He would have to be more careful. Servis had lost a few friends back in the dwarven homeland while demonstrating his new unmanned catapult. Several buildings had been destroyed as well. Yes, he decided, he would have to be more careful. He did not want to lose his good friends Angus Whisperstone and Adaxxis Nightshade. Even the best gremlin cannot invent new friends.

****

The guard outside Lord Jennithos's manor relished his post; the night air blew gently across his face. The moonlight poured gently upon the tiled streets of Blodstad. He never encountered much on his shift. Even with his lord throwing a dinner party inside, the night had been calm so far. He continued his watch, pleased with his efforts, until he noticed a beggar sitting up against the western manor wall. He thought to alert his commander, but decided he could handle this problem on his own. He marched right up to the robed and dirty figure.

"Move on this is not an inn." The guard stated kicking the beggar.

"Please sir, I have no money for a room." The figure bleated weakly.

"Well, take this copper and go find lodging. You can't stay here." The guard reached into his coin purse and preceded to hand the beggar a copper coin. What happened next would be the last thing the guard would remember the next morning, beside a throbbing headache. The beggar moved like the wind, and before the guard could react, his arm was twisted behind his back and he was helpless. There was a sharp pain in his neck and words spoken into his ear he would never forget.

"I let you live for your act of kindness, nothing more," the beggar hissed in a cold whisper. Darkness overtook him soon after. The beggar then dragged the guard to a nearby alley. He removed his dirty robes. The beggar, now adorned in black leather armor, grabbed a set of keys from the unconscious guard and bolted off toward the servant's entrance to the manor. Adaxxis Nightshade loved his work.

***

Lord Jennithos was a wealthy man, and many in Blodstad would love to see him fall. Jennithos's holdings in the trade markets of Blodstad were quite large. He was also a member of the trade commission for the city. The members of the commission knew he was a greedy man. There was a vote on a new trade bill coming up at the next meeting that, if passed, would raise the price of shipping out of Blodstad. The price increase would put many smaller tradesmen out of business and hurt some of the larger firms as well. Jennithos and those like him who also had a stake in the shipping business would profit greatly, and eliminate their competition. Jennithos was the main force behind the creation of the bill. Several days earlier, his counselors had informed him, a few threats had been received on his life. The unknown parties stated they would kill him if he continued to push the new trade bill. Jennithos laughed off their threats, and he boasted to his staff that he was too powerful for such a thing to happen. No one would dare make an attempt upon his life. His council urged him to consider canceling his upcoming dinner party, until the bill was passed and all had settled. Jennithos ignored them and announced to everyone he would not halt the dinner and hide from his enemies.

The dinner party continued as planned, and as Jennithos sat at the head of his large well-set table, he smiled. Next to him on his right sat General Iroths Gregory. He commanded the Blodstad army. Gregory was menacing, silver haired, man in his forties. He despised these La-de-dah parties, but also knew it was good to have the rich on your side when the next elections for his post came about. Jennithos mopped his sweaty brow, and proceeded to belch, much to the general's dismay. The general's steel gray eyes looked upon his bloated host in disgust. General Gregory reasoned, that every lord present felt the larger his waistline, the more powerful he was. Jennithos, by Gregory's reckoning, was the fattest, and most foolish of the lords here. He had heard of the threats on Jennithos's life, yet he still held his little party, not even considering his new enemies might make this his last meal.

***

The assassin breezed across the hall, more like a ghost than a living being. Lost in his own thoughts, a guard mumbled under his breath about nothing ever happening on his shift. Adaxxis grinned in the shadows of a nearby alcove, amused by the guard's remark, some people wish for things they do not really want. The guard continued his pace down the hallway unaware of the danger ahead of him. Adaxxis held his breath; the time for introductions was at hand. The moment before the strike always excited the assassin. It was a game of hunter and prey, and Adaxxis Nightshade was the ultimate hunter. The Cali-benna would be the only thing to save him his fate, and he was not a betting man nor did he worship the god of luck. Suddenly the guard heard a whisper.

"Wish granted little prey." To the guard the voice seemed to echo all about the hall. Adaxxis caught the guard, as he sank from the temporary poison the assassin had injected into his neck. The mixture just put the victim into a deep sleep; this was exactly what assassin desired. He was not being paid for this man's death. Adaxxis dragged the sleeping guard, to the alcove and hid him there. Then he crept silently down the hall to the place from where he would assassinate his Mark.

***

General Gregory listened as his guard whispered the news to him. He thought it strange t some of Lord Jennithos's personal guards were missing from their posts. He sat for a moment considered his options. He was not here this evening to watch over the event and make sure the lord's guards were not playing cards, instead of manning their posts. However, there were still the formalities of his position as leader of the city army to be dealt with. He motioned for his guard to come closer.

"Take a group of men and find those fools, get them back on post before it causes a panic among the guests." Gregory whispered. The guardsman nodded and hurried off to follow his commander's orders. Jennithos noticed the strange look on Gregory's face, and questioned him.

"What was that about, dear sir?" Jennithos ⸱ʔaiting for his guest to answer.

Lordship, my men are just
⸱re not big on formal occasions;

battle is more their style. I told my captain to inform them I would be leaving soon. I would first ask your Lordship's permission, of course," Gregory stated dryly.

"I don't mind if you leave after my speech, which I will be doing after dessert." Jennithos replied, between belches.

The general nodded and once more reminded himself why he needed to be pleasant to men such as Jennithos. The army was his life, and he well paid to be its commander. He would allow his host to keep him there for his boring speech. Gregory considered it a minor cost for the power it purchased.

***

The glass pane gently floated to rest upon another nearby piece of glass. Adaxxis still could up a spell or two when he needed it. The pale crouched on the glass ceiling above the dining hall in Jennithos's manor, looking down into the hole he had created by removing one of the glass panes. His orange eyes scanned those seated at the long dining table. The assassin spotted Jennithos seated at the table's head. A smile crept to the elf's lips. This would be quick and deadly. He pulled out his new handheld crossbow. The lord would fall dead, and the assassin would be gone before anyone knew the better. The Mark was in conversation with a guest seated near him. Adaxxis aimed his crossbow at Jennithos's heart.

"Hold it right there!" A voice boomed, followed by the sound of heavy armor rattling. Adaxxis looked ᵗo see seven well-armed guards, their weapons ᵘnison. The assassin stood and raised his

whip

lf

"Well, who invited you?" Adaxxis smiled and questioned his new friends.

"That is the question I was going to ask you," a guard wearing an ornate breastplate commented drawing closer. Adaxxis fired his crossbow in a blur of movement; the bolt clanged as it was deflected off the guard's helm. The guard screamed as he jumped, sword held high, straight at the assassin.

***

The general heard the scream only seconds before a rain of glass fell upon the dining room table. He opened his eyes to see a figure leap to his feet and his own captain, impaled upon his own sword, lying dead upon the table. The figure held a dagger in each hand, while the guests of Lord Jennithos screamed in panic. The presence of the intruder caused the general to explode with anger.

"You shall die for your crimes this night!" The general screamed, drawing his sword. A dagger ripped through the general's unprotected shoulder, causing him to drop his sword to the floor. The leader of the city's army screamed with pain. Jennithos sat in his chair terrified, and crying like a frightened child.

"General Gregory, I did not expect to see you this night. Are elections so soon?" Adaxxis stated as he leapt at Jennithos. The lord was so stunned he did not even flinch as the assassin landed nearby and placed a dagger at his throat. Jennithos felt his whole world caving in and he looked to Gregory, his eyes tear-filled, and pleading for help. The General regarded the assassin and his victim. How pitiful Jennithos looked as death hovered nearby. None of the guests moved, and suddenly the sound of the dining hall's doors bursting broke the silence, as guards clamored into the room.

"Hold your men, general, or I will slice Jennithos throat before all his guests," the assassin warned. The general looked at the blade creasing the lord's throat. Gregory was no fool. He knew this cloaked being was here to kill Jennithos, but perhaps he could stall. Then he could kill or capture the assassin.

"Hold, stand your ground men and no one in this room move!" The general commanded.

"Well, murderer, you have us at your mercy. What now?" Gregory questioned, stalling, hoping one of his men was smart enough to move archers into place to kill the assassin.

"Nothing, I just came to give Jennithos a message." Adaxxis stated calmly.

"What is that message?" The general asked hoping to give his men more time, if they needed it.

"The message is for Jennithos, not for you, dear general." The assassin smiled.

"Then give him the message." The general hoped his men were now in place.

The Assassin suddenly removed his blade from Jennithos's throat, and put it in his belt. Taking a step away from Jennithos he spoke loud enough for all to hear.

"Lord Jennithos, there are those who feel you should change your mind on the passing of the new trade bill." Adaxxis spoke loudly.

"Well, that is understandable but I assure you, sir, not possible." Jennithos, even looking upon the face of death, was still quite the greedy man.

"That is what they expected you would say nothing personal, my lord." Adaxxis shot back.

"Please, sir, whatever they are paying you I can triple it." Jennithos begged for his life.

"That may be true, but I, too, feel that is not a possibility. I have a contract to complete. May death greet you with open arms Lord Jennithos." Adaxxis moved like a serpent striking his next meal. The assassin's words seemed to finish upon impact of the crossbow bolt in Jennithos's neck. The guests went into mass panic; arrows rained down upon the assassin from the shattered glass ceiling. Gregory's men rushed through the fleeing guests to reach the escaping assassin.

"Kill him now!" Gregory screamed, seeing Jennithos slumped over the table in his own blood.

Adaxxis was too quick. The assassin ran towards an ornate stained glass window. The guards sped after trying desperately to intercept him. The assassin stopped just before the window, turned, and looked at Gregory.

"I am sorry it was not your dinner, to which I was invited. One day, perhaps, dear general." The assassin then jumped, smashing through the stained glass window. The guards arrived at the window seconds after. Peering out they saw the street three stories below filled with glass and nothing more.

"He's gone sir," stated a guardsman upon turning to face Gregory who had just arrived at the window.

"That's impossible. The fall alone would have killed him," Gregory growled, shoving his men out of the way.

Gregory's eyes searched the street below, and he banged his fist in frustration upon the window's ledge. His mind raced as anger rose within his heart. The Assassin had survived the fall. He wouldn't get far though, Gregory reasoned. This unknown assailant had gone too far; he had embarrassed the general in front of the mercantile governing body. Who ever this scoundrel was, he had now purchased Gregory's wrath for a lifetime.

"Go take some men and search the grounds. He must be here somewhere," Gregory raged, turning away from the window.

"I want his head now, so I may watch him hang from the gallows when the sun sets this coming day." The general's face was flushed with an anger few of his regiment had ever seen.

The general fumed, unaware, of an amused audience within earshot. If he only knew how close, his quarry really was. Adaxxis smiled as he hovered just above the window near the general's back leaning against the manor's stone wall. The general, with a sudden click of his boots, stormed off to calm the remaining lords and try to regain some of his bruised reputation. Adaxxis heard Gregory march off muttering to himself and he smirked quietly. The assassin concentrated, spoke a few soft words of magic and floated down to the street below. Adaxxis quickly determined his location and, while in full run, decided which way to evade the growing search of the manor's guards.

***

The guards tramped down the alley next to the manor watched by a beggar seated against the manor's high wall. One of the guards stopped and kicked the beggar. "Have you seen anyone come this way?" the guard demanded. The beggar's filthy pale hands reached out to the guard. "No sir, can you spare some copper?"

"Leave here before I lock you up in the city jail!" he guard responded and ran off to catch up with his group. At the end of the alley, the guard stopped and turned his head, looking back. The beggar was nowhere to be seen. His captain called out to him, and the young guard shouted back. "Just some beggar sir, nothing to worry about." The young guardsman quickly ran off to follow his captain.

A pair of orange eyes watched the guard run off; a set of filthy brown robes fell to the floor. The night air was warming up as dawn approached. A figure smiled in the dark alley, walking deeper into the shadows growing around him. The assassin soon disappeared, leaving the shouts and confusion he had created this night far behind. This would put a damper on any personal appearances he might have considered at any local tavern. Gregory would turn over almost every stone, for a while, to find him. The performance of a Well-known was quite a risky endeavor and the assassin was not concerned by the ripples he had now set into motion within the pool of fate. This was not the first time he had done this type of contract and, Calli-benna willing, it would not be his last.

Adaxxis never thought to fear the future. It brought him comfort, for the unknown is always exciting for those seeking their future in this world, and what a future it would be for the now very popular assassin.

Blossoms

Blossoms of cherry

In spring's bloom

Flowers of doom

Perfumed with anger

Colored with danger

A flowered revenge

A victim's sight

Full of death and fright

Blood upon rice paper

Dishonored the daughter

A father seeks slaughter

For honor, for family name

Upon the bloody paper

Love has anguished word

Death is now absurd

A father's heart shattered

A suitor lies broken and battered

For honor, for family name

Now the house's head

Weeps for the dead

A blade finds a new victim

Dishonored the suitor

A father seeks slaughter

For honor, for family name

Blossoms of cherry

In spring's bloom

Flowers of doom

Now rest, now bless

Family in funeral dress

Weeping upon two graves

~

Harpy

The harpy was ever cruel

Beyond certainty mean

It was her solemn rule

That beauty was obscene

Upon her roost bitter

Full of malice conceived

Her thoughts would slither

In darkness she believed

All the gorgeous butterflies

That fluttered about endlessly

She wished to hear their cries

As she stomped with cruelty

Her squawks were pure terror

Her visage death incarnate

Hate was her eternal lover

In her winter days of late

No one living thing detected

Her missing despicable glare

When death had collected

Her empty soul with care

The roost was silent and empty

No more spiteful cries

All the animals quite happy

To know that evil also dies

~

To the Bridge

A pale moon
The devil's boon
To the bridge
To the bridge
I ride

Headless is he
A soul of treachery
Seeker of my demise
Cursed and tormented
A soul never repented

Will this mare
Get me there
Beyond the axe
That seeks my head
A trophy for the undead

A pale moon

The devil's boon

To the bridge

To the bridge

I ride

The chase is weary

The road bleary

Eyes sting with tears

Away from death

Surpass the breadth

Will this mare

Get me there

Beyond the axe

That seeks my head

A trophy for the undead

A pale moon

The devil's boon

To the bridge

To the bridge

I ride

~

Banshee

She wanders the shore

Singing endlessly of death

A chilling and melancholy score

Filled with undead breath

Does she call?

For the preacher

Or your sister

Perhaps for you

Death is waiting

Life is fading

She cries

She weeps

For the living

Death unforgiving

Hear the Banshee

And her fatal symphony

Under cloak of grey

Black tendrils for hair

As she walks the bay

He voice fills the air

Does she call?

For the preacher

Or your sister

Perhaps for you

Death is waiting

Life is fading

She cries

She weeps

For the living

Death unforgiving

Hear the Banshee

And her fatal symphony

Ships will not anchor

To stay clear of her path

Wicked is her anger

Lethal for all her wrath

Does she call?

For the preacher

Or your sister

Perhaps for you

Death is waiting

Life is fading

She cries

She weeps

For the living

Death unforgiving

Hear the Banshee

And her fatal symphony

~

Devin the Undertaker

Devin the Undertaker
Owns a small cemetery
Being its only caretaker
To him death is just ordinary

At night, Devin gets no rest
From rattle and knock of naked bones
Zombies on trumpet, Ghouls on drum
Banshees wailing in endless drones
It is such a horrid dismal hum

He sees from his window
The undead party and dance
In graveyard filled with eerie glow
Lost in some horrific trance

At night, Devin gets no rest

From rattle and knock of naked bones

Zombies on trumpet, Ghouls on drum

Banshees wailing in endless drones

It is such a horrid dismal hum

Come morning they shall return

To crypt, grave and mausoleum

How Devin does often yearn

That he could join the pandemonium

At night, Devin gets no rest

From rattle and knock of naked bones

Zombies on trumpet, Ghouls on drum

Banshees wailing in endless drones

It is such a horrid dismal hum

~

Dragon's Cave

In the hour of my death
I took my final breath
Face to face with oblivion
In the form of a dragon

I sought to take his treasure
To fulfill my greedy pleasure
Until the beast did awake
Then my life was at stake

His grin was quite scary
My situation quite hairy
I unsheathed my wicked sword
Stood proud upon his monstrous horde

My mind raced for a plan
To save my life if I can

However, dragons are foul tempered
To thieves who have come uninvited

So do I run?
Moreover, make it fun
Give quite a chase
I will die no matter the case

The creature then laughed
I stood quite abashed
Where was humor in this situation?
That seemed to be my extinction

I asked the dragon to spare me
Let this foolish man go free
Tears welled in his reptilian eyes
As he broke into hysterical cries

It was then an odd draft I felt

To my surprise, I had cut my own belt

A most embarrassing blow I had dealt

To my once proud family kilt

Needless to say I lived another day

The Dragon's laughter an endless bay

Too humored by my situation to slay

Humiliation helped me get away

I am not proud of this tale

It is surely worth a mug of ale

So pay up my newfound friend

This tale is at its hilarious end

~

Nursery Rhyme Poker

Three blind mice
Loved to play poker
Dealt were they thrice
Yet never saw a joker

Humpty Dumpty played the best
Built up quite a winning nest
Big Bad Wolf the unscrupulous dealer
Felt the egg's pot should be leaner

Three little pigs pocketed aces
They grinned with greedy faces
Bo-Peep did not play a pair of twos
She had no real desire to lose

Hand by hand did fall
Humpty confident bet it all

Then came the last blind rodent

Who produced a flush quite excellent

A great winner this mammal felt

With a hand he never saw dealt

Sighed did the pigs and Bo-Peep

Their pockets now not so deep

Away with golden jingle

The mice did blindly mingle

Off to buy a pound of cheese

Or simply what ever they please

~

Heimdall

Across the rainbow bridge
Ever alert to sight and sound
The evil ones do ever cringe
To know that his watch abound
Heimdall. Heimdall, Heimdall

The giants in anquish loom
Enemies of hatred and evil
Await the prophecy of doom
Ragnarok, Ragnarok, Ragnarok

Glasheim must be protected
From its halls enemies ejected
Beware of the watcher's song
Waited by god and giant for overlong
Heimdall, Heimdall, Heimdall

In Asgard's dark final hour

The horn of Heimdall sings

Evil shall rise with power

Ragnarok, Ragnarok, Ragnarok

To battle, to war, one and all

Heard by all Heimdall's call

The time of Ragnarok is here

The time of death draws near

The real shall become myth

To fade forever into the mist

Heimdall, Heimdall, Heimdall

~

Sherwood's Robin

Among Sherwood's shadowed trees

The Merry Men collect their fees

The corrupted rich ever should

With care, be aware of Robin Hood

Sherwood's Robin is he

Villain or Hero

What do the people see?

Friar Tuck blesses the bounty

In poor Nottinghamshire county

The wicked and lackey sheriff

Shall never receive ill gotten tariff

Sherwood's Robin is he

Villain or Hero

What do the people see?

Hunted long is this brash robber

Befriended by one Will Scarlet

And his banished courtly lover

Maiden Marion now called harlot

Sherwood's Robin is he

Villain or Hero

What do the people see?

With Little John and Merry Men

Robin seeks Prince John's end

With quiver, bow and arrow

He will end the Poor's sorrow

Sherwood's Robin is he

Villain or Hero

What do the people see?

Noble King Richard shall return
To claim his forgotten throne
Prince John shall soon learn
Robin Hood shall not leave him alone

Sherwood's Robin is he
Villain or Hero
What do the people see?

Among Sherwood's shadowed trees
The Merry Men collect their fees
The corrupted rich ever should
With care, be aware of Robin Hood

~

A Great King

Great Excalibur in stone
Brings boy king to throne
In darkest medieval times
To a land tainted with crimes

Excalibur for King
Wielded by his hand
With crown of golden ring
Both shall command

He builds a glorious realm
Protected by knights in helm
Seated at table equal and round
Pride and power spread around

Excalibur for King
Wielded by his hand

With crown of golden ring

Both shall command

A beautiful Queen secretly obscene

With burning forbidden love unseen

The King's champion her lover

A mighty court destined for disaster

Excalibur for King

Wielded by his hand

With crown of golden ring

Both shall command

An old wizard unwise betrayed

Evil cards dealt by wickedness and played

A bastard child born in darkness cries

A King swallowed by treachery and lies

Excalibur for King

Wielded by his hand

With crown of golden ring

Both shall command

A battle of father and wicked son

Here all things shall come undone

A King dies while son lies slain

So ends the great King's reign

~

Twelve tasks for Zeus's son

By the will of Mycenaean King
Hercules must do these things

Twelve labors for the son of Zeus
To seek his own penance
This deemed his sentence

The Nemean Lion to slay
Bring to the king of Mycenae

Eleven labors for the son of Zeus
To seek his own penance
This deemed his sentence

To destroy the Hydra heads of nine
To make redeemed his crime

Ten labors for the son of Zeus

To seek his own penance

This deemed his sentence

Retrieve the stag with horns of gold

The great son of Zeus was told

Nine labors for the son of Zeus

To seek his own penance

This deemed his sentence

Destroy the terrible Mycenaean boar

See to it that is no more

Eight labors for the son of Zeus

To seek his own penance

This deemed his sentence

Clean now the Augean stables

Perhaps Zeus's son shall be unable

Seven labors for the son of Zeus

To seek his own penance

This deemed his sentence

Destroy the evil Stymphalian birds

These were the king's words

Six labors for the son of Zeus

To seek his own penance

This deemed his sentence

Capture the dread Bull of Crete

Bring this trophy before king's feet

Five labors for the son of Zeus

To seek his own penance

This deemed his sentence

Capture the man-eating mares

Bring them hither if you dare

Four labors for the son of Zeus

To seek his own penance

This deemed his sentence

A girdle from queen of Amazon

Mycenaean king demanded done

Three labors for the son of Zeus

To seek his own penance

This deemed his sentence

Steal the monster Greyon's Cattle

You will not succeed without battle

Two labors for the son of Zeus

To seek his own penance

This deemed his sentence

Gather golden apples from the heavens

This shall be your task eleven

One labor for the son of Zeus

To seek his own penance

This deemed his sentence

Tame great canine Cerberus

Display him before us

All the labors for Zeus's son

Completed his debt now done

Repented and now free

After twelve years of slavery

~

About The Author

Philip Lee McCall II is an avid gamer and reader of Fantasy and Science fiction. He has walked the roads of his imagination for over thirteen years. Writing has always given him a way to express his love for both Fantasy and Science fiction.

When he is not writing a story of the fantastic, he lives quietly with Frances, his muse and wife. They share their magical home in Florida with a Persian named Baby, and two Rat Terriers named Merlin and Gypsy.

Author's Website: www.philipmccallii.com

We would like to thank you for purchase of this product. We hope you enjoy this book and look forward to bringing you many exciting Fantasy and Science Fiction titles in the future to come.

Sincerely,

Mythix Studios Inc.

www.mythixstudios.com

Farewell to You the Reader

Journey back to the mundane

From whence you came

Thank You

Salutations

Danke Schön

Auf Wiedersehen

Jag Tackar

Adjö

Try not to seek closure

It will not happen anyhow

Hope You enjoyed your stay

Be on your way

This book is over

So close it now

~